SHARK
ATTACK!

A SURVIVE! Story

BY JAKE MADDOX

illustrated by Sean Tiffany

text by Eric Stevens

STONE ARCH BOOKS

Impact Books are published by Stone Arch Books
151 Good Counsel Drive, P.O. Box 669
Mankato, Minnesota 56002
www.stonearchbooks.com

Library of Congress Cataloging-in-Publication Data
Maddox, Jake.

    Shark Attack / by Jake Maddox; illustrated by Sean Tiffany.
    p. cm. — (Impact Books. A Jake Maddox Sports Story)
    ISBN 978-1-4342-1210-8 (library binding)
    ISBN 978-1-4342-1404-1 (pbk.)
    [1. Surfing—Fiction. 2. Sharks—Fiction. 3. Shark attacks—
Fiction.] I. Tiffany, Sean, ill. II. Title.
PZ7.M25643Sf 2009
[Fic]—dc22   2008031960

Summary:
Ever since he arrived at his family's rented summer house, Brendan has
been hearing horror stories from all of the locals about sharks in the
water. His new friend and surfing partner, Alex, swears the stories aren't
true, but Brendan can't shake his fear. Then, one day, when Alex and
Brendan are surfing off the coast, Brendan's shark nightmare comes
true in a horrible way.

Creative Director: Heather Kindseth
Graphic Designer: Carla Zetina-Yglesias

1 2 3 4 5 6 13 12 11 10 09 08

TABLE OF CONTENTS

[CHAPTER 1]

Surfing Summer

"Finally," I said to myself. I had spent the last hour looking for the perfect place to surf. "What a lot of wasted time."

But it's important to me to find a nice quiet place. I like to surf by myself, without a bunch of other kids taking the best waves.

At home, I knew the perfect spot. My friend Carlos and I went there almost every morning.

Sometimes we went before school. We got in an hour of surfing before we had to get dressed and head to the bus.

But here, I didn't know my way around. It was my first summer in Rocky Point. My parents rented a house there for four weeks.

Of course, I begged my parents to send me to surfing camp in Hawaii. That's where Carlos was.

"He's probably on the beach in Maui right this second," I muttered to myself. "I bet it's the best surfing in the world."

I looked around at the clear blue sky and bright white sand. Then I looked at the breakers coming in to the beach. "But this is pretty good too," I admitted to myself. "It would have been better if Hannah hadn't come along."

I laughed. Hannah is my annoying little sister. Luckily, she hates surfing almost as much as I hate horseback riding, her favorite thing to do. That meant she wouldn't be bugging me down here at the beach at all. She usually stayed with my parents while I went to the beach.

I took a deep breath, and then ran with my surfboard into the water. The ocean glowed and rippled under the orange sunrise.

When I got about twenty yards out, I dropped the board and jumped onto it, belly first. Then I started paddling.

Farther and farther out I went. Before long, I was in a good spot to pick up some nice waves. I sat on my board and waited for the perfect one.

Then it came. A nice seven- or eight-foot wave. It wasn't huge, but it was a good start for the day. I got up on my feet just in time, bent my knees, and I was off.

It was a pretty nice ride, under the sunrise, my first day in Rocky Point.

I rode it all the way to the beach. It felt like nothing could go wrong.

"Hey, newbie!" someone called out.

I looked up, but the sun was in my eyes.

Whoever was there laughed. It was a mean, nasty laugh. Then he said, "You're at the wrong beach!"

[CHAPTER 2]

Beach Buddy

"Is that right?" I said. It wouldn't have been the first time I'd defended my rights to surf where I wanted.

I shielded my eyes from the sun and moved toward the voice. I tried to walk strong so this guy would know he couldn't push me around. I wasn't very tough, but I was very tall for my age. Sometimes just being tall helped me to get what I want.

"Who says?" I asked.

"I say," the guy replied. I could see him now. He was a little shorter than me, but strong — like a wrestler. He had jet-black hair and was leaning on his board. It was a pretty nice board. It had a sweet painting of a huge red dragon. Whoever did the graphics was really skilled.

My board was a good board too. No fancy graphics at all, just a good board.

"I surf here every morning," the kid said. "And I don't like company at my beach."

Well, I couldn't blame him for that. I felt the same way. But I also couldn't give in that quickly.

"I just got to Rocky Point," I replied, "and this is the best, quietest beach I've seen. So I'm surfing here every morning for the next four weeks."

"Just got here?" the guy said. He laughed and shook his head. "Tourists. What a pain!"

"You live here all year?" I asked. I never knew that people lived in a beach town even in winter.

The kid nodded. "That's right," he said. "I'm out here every day, wearing my wetsuit if I have to. Even before school sometimes during the fall."

I shrugged. "I surf before school back home," I said. "So what?"

The kid looked at me and thought for a minute. "You're pretty good too, huh?" he asked. "Okay. You can surf here."

"Thanks," I replied. "I'm Brendan."

"Alex," he said. "Welcome to Rocky Point. Now let's surf."

So we did. We both paddled out, and together we caught some great waves.

Soon the sun was pretty high. I realized that my stomach was growling.

"Let's make this the last wave," I said to Alex. He was about twenty yards away from me, straddling his board. "I need to have some lunch."

Alex nodded. "I hear that," he said. "I'm starving too. Whoa, look out!"

He got to his feet as a nice wave moved in. I jumped up too and caught the same wave.

"Woo!" Alex hollered as we rode. He did a nice jump off the crest.

"Nice one, Alex," I called to him. "That was great!"

I stopped talking.

Right where Alex hit the water after his jump, I spotted something every surfer fears. There was a tall, sharp fin sticking out of the ocean.

A shark!

[CHAPTER 3]

Mushroom Rock

I made it back to the beach before Alex did.

I had heard before that when a shark bites you, you don't know until you're back on land. That didn't make any sense to me. Wouldn't you feel the huge teeth going into your skin?

Anyway, I thought I should check myself for shark bites. Then I felt stupid for checking. Of course I hadn't been bitten.

Finally, Alex made it back. He shook his head and water flew off of his hair.

I said, "I'm telling you, Alex. I saw a shark."

"You're crazy, Brendan," he replied, toweling off. "Like I said before, I'm out here every morning. I've never seen a shark this close to shore."

I dried myself off and picked up my board. "Then how do you explain the big fin I saw sticking out of the water?" I asked.

Alex shrugged. "Who knows!" he said. "But it wasn't a shark. Trust me."

We started walking down the beach toward the long wooden steps that led up to the road. Now that I was all dried off and the sun was high, it was getting pretty hot out.

"Haven't you ever seen a shark out here?" I asked.

Alex squinted at me. "Sure," he said. "But not close to the beach, like we were."

We reached the top of the steps. Then we started walking along the road into town.

"Where did you see them, then?" I asked. I had a feeling he was joking with me, trying to scare me.

"Way out," Alex replied. "About a hundred yards out — maybe two hundred yards, actually — is Mushroom Rock."

"Mushroom Rock?" I asked.

Alex nodded. "Right," he replied. "It's this crazy rock that looks like a mushroom. Except it's huge! And they say even though the water's very deep out there, if you find Mushroom Rock, you can stand on it."

"You've never been out to Mushroom Rock?" I asked, wondering about how he'd seen a shark.

"Only on my dad's fishing boat," Alex said. "I've seen sharks a couple of times from the boat."

Alex stopped walking. "But like I said, those are way far out," he added. "I'm heading this way. My house is down on the harbor."

I looked down the hill toward the harbor. It was small and there were a bunch of boats docked.

"My family is staying at the beach houses on the hill," I said.

The road to the right climbed steeply between the harbor and the ocean, heading up to the house we were staying in.

"Okay," Alex said. "I guess I'll see you around, at the beach."

I waved goodbye and started climbing the hill toward the beach house. *Maybe Alex was right,* I thought. *Maybe there was no shark.*

But I know I saw something.

[CHAPTER 4]
Lunch of Lies

I dropped my board on the front porch. Then I walked into the house we rented.

"Out here, Brendan!" my dad called when he heard me come in.

I went through the living room and the kitchen and found my family sitting around the little table on the back porch. It looked like they were having hamburgers.

"Did I miss lunch?" I asked.

My mom got up. "Nope," she said. "We just sat down. I'll get you a burger."

I took the last seat at the table, across from Hannah and my dad. My sister glared at me.

"Don't try anything," she said.

"What would I try?" I asked innocently. Then, the moment she looked away, I snatched a french fry off her plate.

"Hey!" she cried.

"What?" I said, the fry still in my mouth.

"That's enough, you two," Dad said.

Mom put a plate in front of me with a hamburger and my own fries. I squirted some ketchup on the plate. Then I dug right in. I was totally starving.

"So, what have you been up to this morning?" Mom asked as she sat down again.

I shrugged. "You know," I said, "just the same old thing. Surfing."

"Woo, hang ten, dude!" Hannah said. She stuck out her tongue at me.

"Did you find a good spot?" Dad asked.

"Did you meet any other surfers?" Mom asked.

"Yes and yes," I replied. "A great spot, and some kid named Alex. He seems okay."

"Think you'll surf with him a lot this summer?" Dad asked. He took a big bite of his burger. Some ketchup dripped and splattered onto his plate.

"Ew, Dad," Hannah said.

"I guess so," I answered my dad.

"Anything exciting happen at the beach this morning?" Mom asked.

I shrugged, and said, "I don't know."

The truth is, I wasn't really listening all that closely. I was thinking about that shark I saw. Or didn't see. And I was trying to decide if I should mention it to my folks.

"Well, I'm glad you're having fun," Mom said. "Both of you." She turned to Hannah. "Hannah," she said, "tell your brother about the horse farm we went to this morning."

"Oh my gosh," Hannah started, but I tuned her out. I didn't like lying to my parents, but if I told them I might have seen a shark, they might not let me surf.

Or they would think I was crazy.

[CHAPTER 5]
Mr. Howard's Sharks

After lunch, I helped my dad clean up. I washed the dishes, and he dried them.

"Say, Brendan," he said as he was drying the dishes. "Would you mind running into town for me?"

"Sure," I answered. "What's up?"

"Nothing big," Dad said. "Just a few groceries to pick up."

"Okay," I said. "Where's the list?"

Dad shook his head. "No list," he said. "Mom called in the order before we ate. Just go in and speak to Mr. Howard, the grocer. He'll have the order ready. It's all paid for and everything."

"Got it," I said. I was already headed toward the front door. "The grocer's name is Mr. Howard. Be right back!"

The walk to town is much nicer than the walk from town to the house we're staying in. The walk to town is all downhill, and you can see the harbor on one side and the ocean on the other as you walk. It was nice out, so I had a good time walking.

Howard's Grocery is right on the corner of Main Street and Harbor Road. If there's a busy center street in the town of Rocky Point, Main Street is it.

The little bell rang as I pushed open the door and walked into the air-conditioned grocery.

The old man at the counter looked up from his crossword puzzle. "Good afternoon," he said.

"Hi," I replied. "I'm here to pick up some groceries."

Mr. Howard looked at me. "Anything in particular?" he said.

"Oh, my mom called our order in earlier," I said.

Mr. Howard smiled. "I see," he said. "What's the name?"

"Leroy," I said. "Gayle Leroy."

"Leroy. Yes, I've got it right here," Mr. Howard said.

He reached behind him and picked up a big cardboard box. He placed it on the counter in front of me.

"Do you need anything else today?" he asked.

I peeked inside the box. There was some bread, eggs, milk, ground beef, and a few vegetables and apples. Nothing too exciting.

"Nope, I guess not," I said.

"Well," Mr. Howard said. He turned around and opened a small fridge behind him. "Why don't you have a small bottle of pop?" he said. "That's a big box, and you've probably got a long walk back."

He handed me a small glass bottle of soda. "Thank you," I said, taking a big gulp.

"You folks have rented a house for the summer, right?" Mr. Howard asked. He opened another bottle of soda for himself.

I nodded.

"Nice place to stay," Mr. Howard said. "You in town long?"

"Four weeks," I replied. "We live a couple hours down the coast, in the city."

"Are you a big surfer, son?" Mr. Howard asked.

I nodded again. "Yup," I said. "I love to surf. I go every day, even back home."

Then I got to thinking, maybe Mr. Howard would know something about sharks.

"Hey, Mr. Howard," I began. "Have you ever . . . are there any sharks around here?"

Mr. Howard tilted his head forward and looked over his glasses at me. "Sharks?" he said. "Well, I've seen a shark or two in my day, sure."

"Really?" I asked.

"Sure I have," Mr. Howard. "I've lived in Rocky Point all my life. One time, when I was about your age, my father and I took out the old rowboat early on Sunday morning."

He took off his glasses and cleaned them with a handkerchief. Then he said, "We went out through the harbor, then swung around the point, right near Mushroom Rock."

"Mushroom Rock?" I asked with a gulp.

"You've heard of it?" Mr. Howard asked.

"Yup," I replied.

Mr. Howard laughed. "Good to know the kids are still calling it by its right name," he said. "We sat up by Mushroom Rock. It's fairly calm up there. And we started to fish. We let our lines hang, and we just relaxed."

He paused a minute and took a sip of his own bottle of soda. "My dad, he got a bite," Mr. Howard continued. "It felt like a big one. I helped him start to bring her in."

He leaned closer in. "But then," he went on in a whisper, "well, it felt like the whole day went cold. Know what I mean?"

I nodded.

"Suddenly," Mr. Howard went on, "the line went limp, like the fish just stopped trying. And the air felt heavy on us. Dad and I looked up and around. That's when we saw them."

"Them?" I asked.

Mr. Howard nodded slowly. "There were ten sharks, if not more, circling Mushroom Rock," he said. "Dad and I just sat, real quiet."

I stood there, breathlessly, for a moment. "So," I said finally, "what happened?"

"Well, I'm standing here, right?" Mr. Howard said with a big laugh. "Those sharks circled us, seemed like forever. But they swam off after a minute or so. Dad and I rowed back around the point. Neither of us said a word about it until we were safely back in the harbor."

"Wow," I said. "That's some story, Mr. Howard."

"And true as the day is long," he said, standing up straight.

I think he could tell I was nervous, because then he said, "But that's Mushroom Rock, a couple hundred yards out. You've got no reason to fear sharks where you kids surf."

Right, I thought to myself as I picked up the box of groceries. *No reason to fear.*

[CHAPTER 6]
Fin Falls

The next morning, I got to the beach right at sunrise. Alex was already there.

"Hey," I said as I came down the steps to the beach.

"Slept in, huh?" Alex joked.

"Very funny," I said.

Alex shrugged. "Anyway, ready to surf?" he asked. "Are you going to risk a shark attack?"

"You're a real comedian, you know that?" I said as I walked into the water with my board. "I'm ready. Are you?"

"Always," Alex replied. We paddled out.

It was a pretty great morning. The waves were kind of mellow, but we caught a lot. So we had quite a few really nice rides.

It was getting close to lunchtime when it happened. I had just done a nice trick off a small crest, and Alex was cheering from the beach.

"Nice one, B," he called. But just then, I wiped out.

"Oooh!" I heard Alex yell. Then he laughed. That didn't bug me, since I was okay and everything. Besides, we always laughed at each other after a wipeout, as long as no one was hurt.

In this case, though, I wasn't laughing.

"Dude," I said as I walked onto the sand. "I wiped out because I saw a fin again!"

"Oh, right!" Alex said. He laughed again. "The shark made you fall."

I shook my head. "I'm telling you, Alex," I insisted. "I saw a shark!"

"Whatever," Alex replied. Then he ran with his board into the surf to catch one more wave before we left for lunch.

I dropped my board on the sand and sat down. I watched Alex sit and wait a minute, then catch a small wave to ride back.

He was right on the break when he suddenly waved his arms and lost his footing. Wipeout.

Just like me, when he came up to the beach, carrying his board, he wasn't laughing.

"What happened to you?" I asked.

"I saw it too!" he replied. "I saw the fin!"

[CHAPTER 7]

My Bad Mood

"See?" I said. "I told you!"

Alex shook his head. "I don't know," he said. "I still don't know if it was a shark."

"What else could it be?" I shouted. "A big tuna?"

"It could be a dolphin," Alex replied, totally serious. "Really. I used to see dolphins around here all the time. Not in a while, though."

"Come on," I said. I was sure it had been a shark.

Alex shook his head again. "Man, with all the garbage you're talking about sharks today," he said, "I'm probably just seeing things. You probably put it into my head and freaked me out."

"What?" I said. "No way."

"Yes way," Alex said, toweling off. "I bet there was no fin. Just my mind playing tricks on me."

* * *

That whole afternoon I felt kind of mad at Alex. I was still mad later that day, when my dad came into my room.

Does Alex think I'm crazy? I thought, lying on my bed, still in my swim trunks. *That I'm just making it up?*

I was feeling pretty grumpy when my dad asked me to get dressed for dinner.

"Where are we going?" I asked. I didn't feel like putting on pants and a shirt just for some crummy meal out.

"The seafood restaurant on the harbor," Dad replied. "And please, no attitude. Mom and I are excited to try it."

I rolled my eyes as my dad left the room. *Great*, I thought, *a boring dinner at a boring restaurant.*

I had to wear pants and a shirt that Mom had packed for me. Then we headed to town.

I had to admit the restaurant was nice, though. And we sat on an outdoor patio right on the water. Plus they had fish tacos on the menu, so that was cool.

Hannah wanted spaghetti and meatballs.

"It's a seafood restaurant," I said to her. "They don't have spaghetti and meatballs."

But the waiter overheard us. He smiled at Hannah.

"Don't worry, sweetheart," he said. "I'll talk to the chef for you. Would you like that?"

"Yes, please," Hannah said it her cutest voice. I almost puked.

But the tacos were good, and at least Hannah wasn't complaining. She got her spaghetti and meatballs.

By the time dessert came, I was in a much better mood. Then Dad had to go and ruin it.

"How was the surfing today, Brendan?" he asked.

I immediately thought about that fin again, and about Alex saying it never happened.

"I don't know," I answered my dad. "Fine, I guess."

"Doesn't sound fine," Mom said. "You sound upset about it."

I shrugged. "I don't know," I started. "Mr. Howard said something about sharks."

"Sharks?" Dad said, a little too loud.

"Oh my gosh," Hannah said. Her face went totally white. "There are sharks here?"

She looked like she expected a great white shark to walk into the restaurant and eat her and her meatballs that very second.

"I think you're safe at the moment," I said, rolling my eyes.

"Mr. Howard said there were sharks here?" Mom asked.

I nodded. "I've been a little worried about it," I said. "I mean, maybe it isn't safe to surf."

Mom looked confused. "That's the oddest thing," she said. "I spoke to Mr. Howard yesterday, when I ordered those groceries. He told me surfing in Rocky Point is very safe. There hasn't been a shark attack in over fifty years, he said."

"Fifty years?" I asked.

Mom nodded and sipped her coffee. "Right," she said. "Well, except up by Mushroom Rock, according to Mr. Howard, but that's like a mile out."

Funny, I thought. *Mushroom Rock seems to be getting farther and farther away from the beach every time someone mentions it.*

"That reminds me, Brendan," Dad said. He waved at the waiter to get the check. "I heard on the radio that we're expecting a big storm tomorrow afternoon."

"Oh yeah?" I asked.

Dad nodded and pulled out his wallet. "Yeah," he said. "So be careful tomorrow morning. If you see the sky go dark, or if it rains even a single drop, you come right back to the house. Got it?"

"Got it," I said.

[CHAPTER 8]
Undertow

"Hello again," Alex said when I reached the beach the next morning.

"Hi," I said. I guess I was still annoyed with him.

"Sorry about yesterday, man," he said. "I have to admit, I was a little freaked out by that fin."

"That's okay," I replied. "Then you saw it, for sure?"

Alex shrugged. "I must have," he said. "I mean, I'm not crazy, right?"

"Hey, I just met you," I said, putting my hands up. "You could be a total nut for all I know."

He laughed. "All right," he said, heading toward the water. "Are we going to stand here all day, or are we going to surf?"

"Surf!" I said.

"Good," Alex replied. "You know, there's a storm coming in, so we have to get in as many rides as we can."

"That's right! Let's go," I replied, and we both ran into the surf.

It was a great morning. When a storm was coming, even when it was still far off, the waves were really cool.

Yesterday's calm waves were nothing compared to the monsters we were catching that day.

We both wiped out more than we normally do, but it was worth it for the great rides we had in between falls.

"Woo!" Alex yelled as he got up on a high crest.

"Nice one," I called over to him. Then I tried for a 360 and totally blew it.

Alex laughed. "Nice one to you too!" he said jokingly.

We got to the beach and looked out over the water. We could hardly even spot the sun through the low gray clouds.

I looked up at the sky. "It's getting bad now," I said.

"Think we should call it quits?" Alex asked.

"I don't know," I replied. "The storm still looks a few miles out. Let's do one more ride."

"Okay," Alex said. "These waves are too nice to walk away from too soon!"

So we paddled out one more time. The waves coming in looked even bigger than before. Paddling through the rough ocean got harder and harder.

Alex and I looked at each other. "Maybe this is a bad idea," I said.

Alex nodded. "Agreed," he said. "Let's head back."

But it was too late. We tried to turn around and body surf in, but the undertow had us.

For every ten yards we made it toward shore, the ocean pulled us about thirty yards farther out.

"Brendan!" Alex yelled over the noise of the surf. "How are we going to get back to shore?"

"Haven't you ever been caught in the undertow before?" I shouted to him. "We'll be fine. We just have to catch one and ride it in."

"If you say so," Alex said. He looked scared.

"Be ready," I said. I looked over my shoulder for a wave we could catch.

Just then, though, I felt my board scrape bottom. "How could that be?" I muttered to myself. "Why is the water so shallow here? It doesn't make sense."

I rolled off my board and found I could stand up easily. The water was barely up to my knees.

Alex looked over. His face went white. Then he, too, got off his board and slowly stood up.

"This is weird," I said, holding my board.

Alex shook his head. "This isn't weird," he said. "It's bad. Very bad. Do you know where we are?"

"No," I replied.

"This," Alex said nervously, "is Mushroom Rock."

CHAPTER 9

Stranded

"Mushroom Rock?" I cried. "The Mushroom Rock that has all the sharks?"

Alex nodded. "That's the only Mushroom Rock I know," he said.

I looked out over the water toward the beach. We could easily have been two or three hundred yards out.

"I can't believe how far we got pulled," I said.

It was weird to be standing up so far out from shore. "How will we ever get back?" I asked nervously.

"I'm not even worried about getting back," Alex said. "I'm just worried about sharks."

"So what are we going to do?" I asked. I was starting to panic a little.

"Only one thing we can do," Alex replied. "Get on our boards, and paddle like mad!"

"We'll never make it like that," I said.

"Do you have a better idea?" Alex snapped.

Suddenly his eyes went wide and he pointed behind me.

"Look!" he yelled.

I turned to where he was pointing. There, as plain as day, was a tall sharp fin, sticking out of the water. This time there was no doubt. That was a shark.

"It's between us and the beach," I said. "I'm not risking paddling around a shark. I'd rather just stay here on the rock!"

"Maybe we can make it around the point," Alex said.

"To the harbor?" I replied.

"There will be lots of boats coming into the harbor, because of the storm coming in," Alex pointed out. "If we just get to the point, one of them will see us."

I nodded. "Okay," I said. "Let's go for it."

We both held on to our boards and jumped off the rock. We headed in the opposite direction of the beach.

I tried to look over my shoulder for the fin, but I didn't see anything.

The point was another hundred yards past Mushroom Rock. Then the harbor was around it to the right.

I kept my eyes on the point and paddled as hard as I could. Alex was stronger than me. He was a few yards ahead.

Every so often, in the choppy water against the rocks, one of us fell off our board. We scrambled back on and kept paddling as fast as we could.

One time, when I fell off, I felt a little tug on my foot. I tugged back and got right back on my board. Then I kept on paddling toward the harbor.

Alex was beginning to get very far ahead of me. I tried to speed up.

"Alex," I called out. My voice sounded weak. "Wait up for me."

I saw Alex look back over his shoulder. Then he turned his board around and paddled back to me.

I felt like I was being sucked into a whirlpool. For a moment, I closed my eyes.

"You'll be all right, B," Alex said. He sounded miles away. "We're almost around the point. I can see some fishermen coming into the harbor."

I tried to reply, but I couldn't.

"Hey!" Alex yelled. "Over here!"

Then I blacked out.

[CHAPTER 10]
Safe at Last

When I woke up, I was in a weird white bed in a weird white room. My mom and dad were sitting there with Hannah. Mom was crying a little. Alex was standing in the doorway.

"What happened?" I said.

Dad came rushing to my side. "You're all right, son," he said. "You're perfectly safe now."

"Oh, my baby!" Mom cried out, throwing her arms around my neck. Even Hannah came over and kissed my cheek and hugged me.

It took me a few seconds to remember what happened, but when I looked down at my foot, all bandaged up, it all came back to me.

So, what was that tug on my foot? That was a shark bite, of course.

I'd heard people say before that when a shark bites you, you don't even know you're bitten until you're back on land. I always thought that was crazy. But now I get it.

It had felt like someone was just tugging on my leg, like Hannah being a brat in a pool, just to annoy me.

I was lucky that I was with Alex. I don't think I would have made it around the point on my own.

Thanks to him, I was on a fishing boat within minutes, and at the hospital pretty soon after that. Dr. Brass in the emergency room gave me about a million stitches, but he said I'd be fine soon. I'd even be able to surf again the next summer.

And believe me, when my family went back to Rocky Point next year, I made Alex surf with me at the crowded beach, as far from Mushroom Rock as possible.

ABOUT THE AUTHOR

Eric Stevens lives in St. Paul, Minnesota. He is studying to become a middle-school English teacher. Some of his favorite things include pizza, playing video games, watching cooking shows on TV, riding his bike, and trying new restaurants. Some of his least favorite things include olives and shoveling snow.

ABOUT THE ILLUSTRATOR

When Sean Tiffany was growing up, he lived on a small island off the coast of Maine. Every day, from sixth grade until he graduated from high school, he had to take a boat to get to school. When Sean isn't working on his art, he works on a multimedia project called "OilCan Drive," which combines music and art. He has a pet cactus named Jim.

GLOSSARY

crest (KREST)—the top of a wave

docked (DOKD)—if a boat or ship is docked, it is tied up to keep from moving away from shore

fin (FIN)—a part on the body of a fish shaped like a flap that is used for moving and steering through the water

graphics (GRAF-iks)—art and designs

harbor (HAR-bur)—a place where ships shelter or unload their cargo

point (POINT)—a part of land that sticks out into a body of water

rented (RENT-id)—paid money to borrow

shallow (SHAL-oh)—not deep

skilled (SKILLD)—very good at something

tourists (TOOR-ists)—people who are visiting a place

undertow (UHN-dur-toh)—a strong current under the surface of a body of water

wetsuit (WET-soot)—a garment worn in the water to keep a swimmer or surfer warm

MORE ABOUT
SHARK SAFETY

If you swim or surf in waters where sharks may be present, remember these tips and stay safe:

- Always surf or swim with a friend.

- Stick to areas patrolled by lifeguards. They watch out for sharks and provide assistance after an attack.

- Swimming at dawn, dusk, and night can be dangerous. This is when sharks move closer to shore to feed.

- If you have an open sore or are bleeding, stay out of the water. Sharks are attracted to blood.

- Avoid murky waters, which are popular spots for sharks.

- Don't wear shiny jewelry. When it reflects, it looks like a fish scale to a shark.

- Stay away from swimwear that uses contrasting colors, such as yellow and dark blue. Sharks can see these color combinations extremely well.

- Lots of splashing might be fun. But sharks seem to swim toward this action.

- If you notice fish or sea turtles swimming off suddenly, leave the water. They may know something you don't know.

DISCUSSION QUESTIONS

1. In this book, Brendan is attacked by a shark. Do you know other books, movies, or real-life stories about shark attacks? Talk about them.

2. At first, Alex didn't seem to like Brendan. Why did that change? What are some things you can do if someone doesn't like you?

3. In this book, did Alex and Brendan do anything wrong? If you were with them, what would you have done differently? Talk about your answers.

WRITING PROMPTS

1. Brendan wanted to go to surfing camp with his best friend, but instead, his parents rented a house near a beach. Write about your idea of a perfect summer vacation. Where would you go? What would you do? Who would you be with?

2. Brendan says that his sister is annoying. Write about one of your siblings. If you don't have one, write about the sibling of someone you know.

3. Try writing chapter 9 from Alex's point of view. What does he see and hear? What does he think about? How is his experience different from Brendan's?

INTERNET SITES

Do you want to know more about subjects related to this book? Or are you interested in learning about other topics? Then check out FactHound, a fun, easy way to find Internet sites.

Our investigative staff has already sniffed out great sites for you!

Here's how to use FactHound:

1. Visit *www.facthound.com*

2. Select your grade level.

3. To learn more about subjects related to this book, type in the book's ISBN number: **9781434212108**.

4. Click the **Fetch It** button.

FactHound will fetch the best Internet sites for you!